Yusuf's Ramadan Lantern

Story by Jasmin Zine
Illustrations by Brad Cornelius

Story
Jasmin Zine

Illustrations
Brad Cornelius

Book Design
Robinson Design
Aliuddin KhaJa

ISBN# 1-156316-508-2
LLC:

Printed in India

IQRA' International Educational Foundation
7450 Skokie Blvd.
Skokie, IL 60077 USA
Tel: 1-847-673-4072
Fax: 1-847-673-4095
E-mail: iqrapdc@aol.com

Dedication:

To my sons Yusuf and Usama Zine for their love and support.
May you always cherish the traditions of your family and faith.

Acknowledgements:

My thanks to Leila Maarouf for sharing with me the history and
significance of the fanooz and to Suzanne Muir whose
friendship and collaboration made writing this story possible.

I was so excited that I could barely stand still. At long last a whole month had passed and my grandparents were coming back from Egypt. They had been visiting our relatives in Cairo. Yesterday my grandfather called to tell me he was bringing home a very special surprise for me! He said it was a secret, but I already knew what it was going to be.

Before he left, I had asked my grandfather to buy me a new electronic fanooz lantern. These lanterns were really cool! They looked like old-fashioned lanterns, but had real light bulbs instead of candles and if you pressed a button they even sang a song to celebrate the beginning of Ramadan. I had wanted one ever since my friend Usama brought one back from his trip.

I couldn't wait to see my grandfather and thank him for the gift!

Finally I heard the doorbell ring and I quickly scrambled over to open the door. My grandfather stood there smiling down at me holding a cardboard box. My grandmother bent over to give me a big hug as she and my grandfather came inside. I held my grandfather's hand as he came in the room. He bent down and hugged me saying, "Ramadan Mubarak, may the blessings of Ramadan be upon you, my son."

My grandparents sat down and told us about the wonderful time they had spent in Egypt visiting family and friends. They showed us pictures of them standing by the pyramids and drinking tea underneath date trees.

My grandfather could tell I was getting anxious as I began fidgeting in my chair. He smiled and took me by the hand out to the back porch, carrying the strange cardboard box under his arm.

We sat down on the porch swing and my grandfather said, "I think you are getting anxious to know about the surprise I got you."

"Oh I already know what it is Grandpa – it's a fanooz!" I replied excitedly. "Well, how did you guess?!" my grandfather laughed as he carefully opened the cardboard box.

When I saw what he held in his hand I felt a look of disappointment slowly cross my face. Instead of a brand new ultra-cool electronic fanooz, he held an old metal lantern with cracked, yellow glass.

"Grandpa!" I exclaimed, "Is this some kind of joke? Where is my electronic fanooz?"

"Oh Yusuf, my son," he said. "This is a very special fanooz. Did you know that this used to be mine when I was your age?"

I settled back on the swing as it softly rocked back and forth and my grandfather told me the story of his fanooz.

"When I was a boy," he began, "there was no electricity in our village so when Ramadan came we did not have alarm clocks to wake people up before dawn so they can eat before beginning their fast. Instead, the men in our village

would take turns staying awake and then as the time of

Fajr in the early morning hours approached, they would

light a special fanooz lantern and head out to wake their

neighbors."

"I remember when it was my father's turn to wake the village. He would very softly tap my shoulder and whisper for me to wake up and bring his drum.

I would rub my eyes awake and feel around in the dark until

I felt the smooth surface of the drum beside my bed."

"We would then head out in the darkness with my father

carrying his drum while I held the fanooz up high so

we could see the way to our neighbors' homes. As we

approached, my father began to softly pound a beat on

his drum. Gradually the beat became louder and louder

and then he would sing out to the hushed night, 'Wake up, wake up, it's time for suhoor! Wake up! Wake up and share blessings saved for those who eat in the early hours before light. Surely this is the month of generosity and reward!'"

"Sometimes my cousins would come out and join us,

banging on metal pots with a stick and together we all would

sing 'Ahlan, ahlan, yaa Ramadan!' 'Welcome, welcome, oh

Ramadan!' It was a very special and joyous time!"

"Then we would hurry back to our home before the white thread of light appeared in the dawn sky to eat suhoor with our family. We ate dates soaked in milk and had fresh bread

with fava beans that my mother prepared. We ate together

until we heard the call to prayer echoing into our house."

I looked at the expression of happiness that came over my grandfather's face as he told me this story. I knew then that the old and cracked lantern he had brought me was better than any fancy new ultra-cool fanooz lantern with flashing light bulbs and electronic tunes.

I hugged my grandfather and thanked him for the very special gift. I felt proud that he wanted me to have something so wonderful!

As we got up to go back inside, my grandfather turned to me and said with a sly smile, "By the way Yusuf, I almost forgot, I have something else for you." He reached inside the big pockets of his overcoat and pulled out a box wrapped in shiny green and white paper. I teared off the wrapping paper and opened the box. To my surprise, inside I saw the fancy new fanooz I had been asking for! But somehow I wasn't as excited as I thought I would be.

"What's wrong, Yusuf?" my grandfather asked when he saw my expression, "I thought this was what you really wanted."

"It's nice," I told him, "but I like the other one better. It's old and the glass is cracked, but when I look at it, I'll always remember how you used to carry it at night when you were a boy just like me."

I always keep that old lantern in my room where I can see it at night. My dad has fixed the cracked glass and we polished it up nice and shiny. In the early morning hours during Ramadan we light a candle inside it when we wake up to eat. As I gaze at the candle, I imagine my grandfather as a young boy like me carrying the fanooz, while his father plays a drum to wake up the village before dawn. I see the images of him dancing in the flame of the candle and the shadows it casts on the wall. And so I am glad that this old lantern has once again become a part of our family!